— For my dear friends, with love. Special thanks also to Manli Peng and Kate Wilson whose help and encouragement was greatly appreciated. W.M.

— To Susan Hou, for all her help. R.K.

Illustrations copyright © 1998 by Wenhai Ma
English text copyright © 1998 by Robert Kraus
Chinese text copyright © 1998 by Debby Chen

Published in the United States of America by
Pan Asian Publications (USA) Inc.
29564 Union City Blvd., Union City, CA 94587

Tel. (510) 475-1185   Fax (510) 475-1489

ISBN 1-57227-045-4
Library of Congress Catalog Card Number: 97-80552

Editorial and production assistance: William Mersereau, Art & Publishing Consultants

Printed in Hong Kong

THE MAKING of MONKEY KING

小石猴稱王

Retold by Robert Kraus and Debby Chen
Illustrated by Wenhai Ma

English / Chinese

Pan Asian Publications

Long, long ago, by the far eastern land of Ao-lai
was a great sea. And out of this swirling sea rose
Flower Fruit Mountain. At the top of this
mountain lay a giant mysterious rock.

很久、很久以前，在遙遠的東方有個傲來國。傲來國靠
近大海，海裏有一座山，名叫花果山，山上開滿了花花
果果，山頂還有一塊奇妙的大石頭。

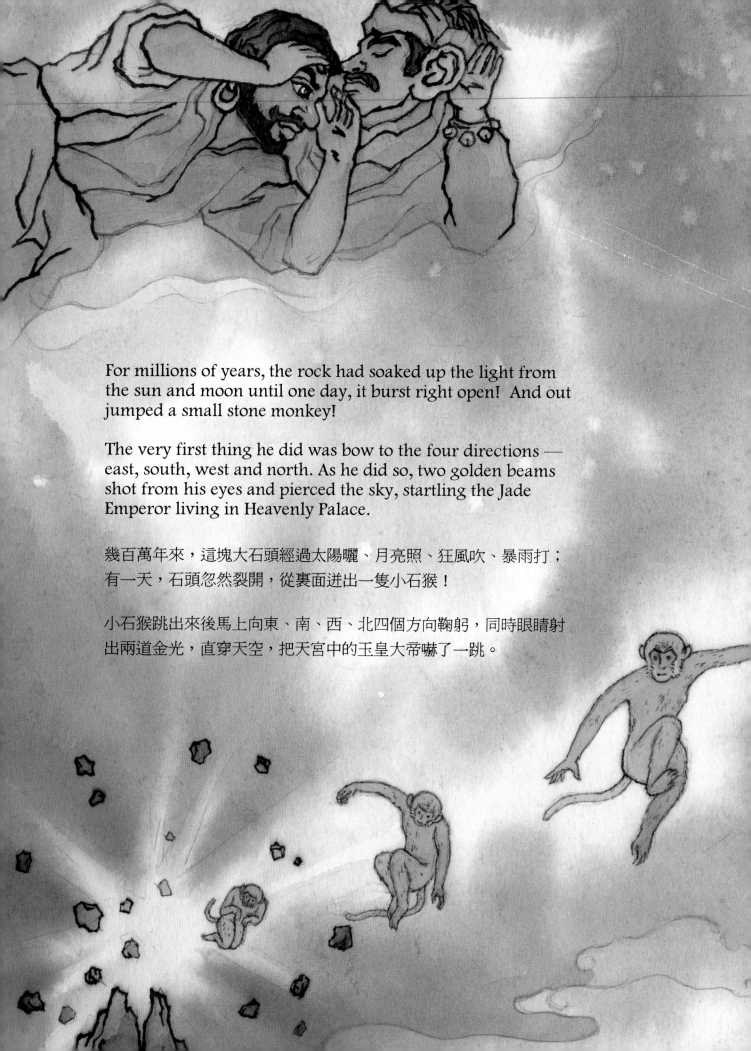

For millions of years, the rock had soaked up the light from the sun and moon until one day, it burst right open! And out jumped a small stone monkey!

The very first thing he did was bow to the four directions — east, south, west and north. As he did so, two golden beams shot from his eyes and pierced the sky, startling the Jade Emperor living in Heavenly Palace.

幾百萬年來，這塊大石頭經過太陽曬、月亮照、狂風吹、暴雨打；有一天，石頭忽然裂開，從裏面迸出一隻小石猴！

小石猴跳出來後馬上向東、南、西、北四個方向鞠躬，同時眼睛射出兩道金光，直穿天空，把天宮中的玉皇大帝嚇了一跳。

The Emperor quickly called his two captains, Thousand Mile Eye and Fair Wind Ear, to investigate. They threw open the South Gate of Heaven, spotted the stone monkey, and quickly reported back to the Jade Emperor who merely nodded, saying, "Since all creatures on earth are magical, this stone monkey should really be no surprise to us."

玉皇大帝立刻召見千里眼和順風耳兩名大將，要他們去探個究竟。他們打開南天門，看到一隻小石猴，馬上回報玉皇大帝。玉皇大帝點點頭說：「世上萬物都是奇妙的，我們不必爲這隻小石猴大驚小怪。」

The stone monkey soon joined the other monkeys who lived on the mountain. Together they spent many joyful days frolicking among wild flowers and feasting on fruit. One hot day, the monkeys went to bathe in a cool, rushing stream. Restless and curious as ever, they all decided to find out where the stream began.

小石猴不久就和山上的猴子們玩熟了；他們快樂地在野花中玩耍、吃各種水果。一個大熱天，猴子們在清涼的激流中洗澡，一時玩興和好奇心大起，他們決定去尋找激流的源頭。

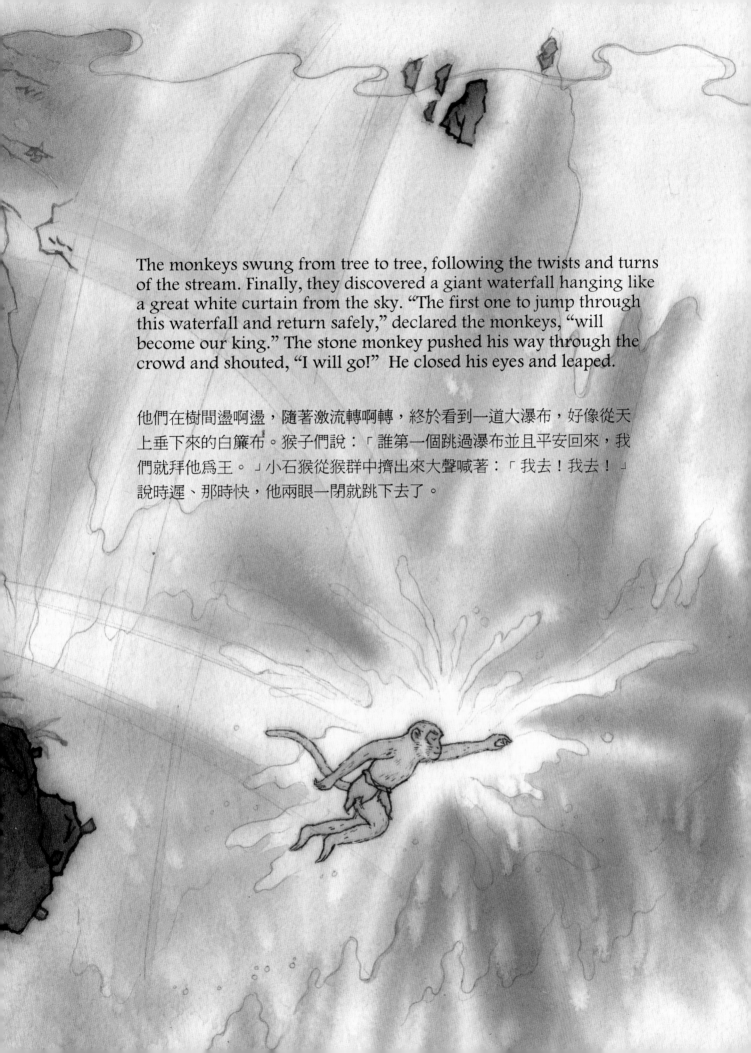

The monkeys swung from tree to tree, following the twists and turns of the stream. Finally, they discovered a giant waterfall hanging like a great white curtain from the sky. "The first one to jump through this waterfall and return safely," declared the monkeys, "will become our king." The stone monkey pushed his way through the crowd and shouted, "I will go!" He closed his eyes and leaped.

他們在樹間盪啊盪，隨著激流轉啊轉，終於看到一道大瀑布，好像從天上垂下來的白簾布。猴子們說：「誰第一個跳過瀑布並且平安回來，我們就拜他為王。」小石猴從猴群中擠出來大聲喊著：「我去！我去！」說時遲、那時快，他兩眼一閉就跳下去了。

When he opened his eyes, he saw a splendid iron bridge stretching before him. Beside the bridge was an inscription that read: *Flower Fruit Mountain is Blessed, and Water Curtain Cave Leads to Heaven.*

Walking boldly over the bridge, the stone monkey soon found a great cave. Inside, there were stone chairs and beds, and hundreds of stone bowls and pots. "What a perfect place to live!" he thought, and he raced back to fetch his friends. Eagerly, they followed him back through the waterfall.

當他睜開眼睛時，他看到一座壯觀的鐵橋橫亙在他面前。橋邊有一塊石碑寫著：「花果山福地，水濂洞洞天」。

小石猴勇敢地走過鐵橋，馬上發現一個大山洞；洞內有石床、石椅，和上百個石鍋、石碗。「這真是個好地方！」小石猴驚嘆一聲，立刻回去告訴朋友們，大家興高采烈地跟著他跳過瀑布到山洞去。

The stone monkey seated himself on the biggest chair. Raising a paw, he declared, "We agreed that whoever jumped through the falls shall be king. So now you must salute me!" "Hurrah! Long live the Handsome Monkey King!" cheered the rest of the monkeys.

Life was now better than ever! During the day they played on Flower Fruit Mountain and during the night they slept in Water Curtain Cave. They no longer worried about harsh weather or fearsome beasts!

小石猴坐在最大的椅子上，舉起手說：「大家說過跳過瀑布的就是大王，所以現在你們要稱我為王！」「萬歲！萬歲！美猴王萬萬歲！」猴子們一齊歡呼。

現在他們的生活過得舒服多了！白天他們在花果山玩，晚上睡在水濂洞，不怕壞天氣也不怕兇猛的野獸！

For four hundred years they lived this carefree life, until one day, during a jolly banquet, a sad thought struck Monkey King and he suddenly burst into tears. "Why are you crying, your Majesty?" asked the bewildered monkeys. "Isn't our life wonderful?" "Life is wonderful," wailed Monkey King, "but one day I will die and this wonderful life will be all over!" Upon hearing this, all the other monkeys burst into tears as well. Finally, a wise old gibbon came forward. "Never fear," he said, "I have heard that Buddhas, Immortals and Sages are not subject to Yama, the God of Death. Why not find these great beings and ask them for the secret to eternal life?"

他們就這樣無憂無慮地過了四百年。有一天，當大家在宴會中玩得正高興，美猴王忽然一陣傷感，哭了起來。「大王，您為什麼哭呢？」猴子們都不明所以地問：「這樣好的生活您還有什麼不滿意？」「我不是不滿意，」美猴王悲嘆著：「可是總有一天我會死去，這些美好的日子就沒有了。」聽了這些話，別的猴子也哭了。這時候一隻年長的長臂猿上前說：「不要怕，我聽說佛、仙、神是不會死的，大王為什麼不去問他們長生不死的秘訣呢？」

Monkey King was overjoyed! The very next day he said good-bye to the other monkeys and set out on his journey in a tiny raft.

美猴王非常高興！第二天一早，他向猴子們說了再見，就坐上小木筏出海去找神仙。

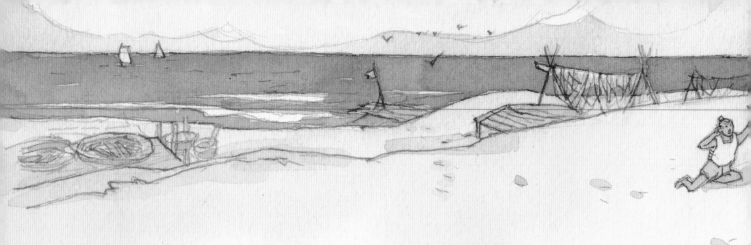

He sailed in and out of sunny days and moonlit nights until he came to a small seaside village. Some fishermen were on the beach, salting their catch. Monkey King noticed with envy that they all wore clothes. He jumped up and down and made such awful faces that all the fishermen ran away in fright. In his haste, one fisherman ran right out of his clothes! This suited the cheeky monkey just fine. He dressed himself in the clothes and set off into the land of humans, proud as a peacock.

他在海上漂啊漂，看著太陽東昇、月亮西沉，終於到了海邊一座小漁村。海邊有幾個捕魚人在醃魚，美猴王看見他們穿著衣服很羨慕。他跳上跳下對著漁夫做鬼臉，把漁夫都嚇跑了。哈！哈！有一個人在慌亂中丟下了衣服。這太好了！調皮的美猴王穿上人的衣服，大搖大擺走進村莊，像孔雀一樣得意洋洋。

Monkey King traveled for many years, asking everyone he met if they knew the whereabouts of a Buddha, an Immortal, or even a Sage. But no one knew. Then one day, he happened upon a woodcutter at the edge of a forest. The woodcutter told him that, indeed, he knew of a magical Immortal named Master Subodhi who lived in a nearby cave with his many students.

他走了好多年，到處向人打聽哪裡有佛祖和神仙，可惜沒有人知道。
有一天，他在森林遇到一名樵夫，樵夫告訴他在不遠的山洞裡，住著
一位神奇的仙人菩提祖師，他收了許多徒弟。

The Master, strange to say, seemed to be expecting Monkey King. And wasting no time, Monkey King asked him if he could become his student. Subodhi looked deeply into his face and replied, "I know you are sincere, and that you have traveled far to find me, but I see also that you are vain and naughty!" "Oh no, I'm not!" protested the Monkey King. "Please, give me a chance!" Subodhi finally relented, "Very well," he said, "you may be my student. While you study with me, you will be known as *Sun Wukong.*"

說也奇怪，菩提祖師好像也在等美猴王來找他呢！美猴王一看見菩提祖師就跪下要拜他爲師。菩提祖師仔細看著他的臉說：「你千里跋涉來找我，一定很誠懇，但是我擔心你又調皮、又愛出風頭。」「不！我不會！」美猴王急著辯說，「請給我一次機會！」菩提祖師終於心軟了，他說：「好吧！我收你爲徒弟。當你在我這裏學習的時候，你的名字就叫『孫悟空』。」

Sun Wukong lived humbly like the other students. He listened intently to Subodhi's teachings and learned the martial arts. Seven long years passed, but he was still no closer to learning the secret for eternal life. Sun Wukong could stand it no longer. In the middle of a class, he jumped up and cried, "This is just too boring! I have been here so long and all I have learned to do is clean, cook and wash." Master Subodhi was furious! He stepped off the podium and struck Sun Wukong three times with his ruler. "You don't want to learn this! You don't want to learn that!" he said, "What do you want to learn?" With that, Master Subodhi left the room, hands crossed behind his back.

孫悟空像其他學生一樣規規矩矩過生活，用心聽課，學習武功。可是七年悠悠度過，他仍然不知道怎樣才會長生不死。一天在課堂上他再也忍不住，就跳起來大喊：「真無聊！我在這裡這麼久，只是清掃、做飯、洗衣。」菩提祖師很生氣，他走下講台，用戒尺在孫悟空頭上打了三下。「你這個不學！那個不學！你到底要學什麼？」菩提祖師隨後走出教室，雙手交叉在背後。

At three o'clock the next morning, Sun Wukong entered Master Subodhi's cave through the back door and knelt beside his bed. Suddenly awakened, Subodhi cried, "What are you doing here?" Sun Wukong replied, "When you struck me on the head three times, that was a sign that I must visit you at three o'clock. And when you put your hands behind your back, that was a sign that I must come in through the back door." Sun Wukong understood the secret signs! Master Subodhi decided that he was indeed ready to learn the Immortal Secrets. He whispered the sacred verses into Wukong's ear, then sent him back to his own cave to practice. Three years later, Subodhi also taught him the Seventy-Two Transformations. Now, he could change into almost anything!

第二天凌晨三點鐘，孫悟空從後門進入菩提祖師的洞室。他跪在床邊，動也不敢動。普提祖師忽然醒來，叫道：「你在這裡做什麼？」孫悟空回答：「您在我頭上打三下，就表示三點鐘；您把手放在背後，就表示要我從後門進來。」孫悟空真聰明！他可以學習最難的長生秘訣了。菩提祖師在他的耳邊輕輕唸出一連串密語，要他回去好好練習。三年後，孫悟空又學會七十二變。現在他能隨心所欲，無所不變了。

One evening, when everyone was out admiring the new moon, Subodhi asked Sun Wukong how his studies were going. "Very well," he replied, "I've already mastered the art of cloud-soaring." Trying to impress his master, he flew into the clouds, traveled four miles and was back in a wink. "That was not cloud-soaring," laughed Subodhi, "that was only cloud crawling! Real cloud-soaring means you can fly a thousand miles with one jump!" "That's impossible!" cried Sun Wukong. "Nothing is impossible, only the mind makes it so," replied Subodhi. He leaned forward and whispered the spell for cloud-soaring. In no time, Sun Wukong mastered it.

一天晚上，當大家在外面賞月時，菩提祖師問：「悟空，你的功夫學得怎麼樣了？」孫悟空說：「很好，我已經學會了筋斗雲。」為了表現他的本事，他衝入雲中飛了四里，一轉眼又飛回來了。「那不是筋斗雲，」菩提祖師笑道：「那是爬雲！真正的筋斗雲可以一個筋斗飛出十萬八千里！」「怎麼可能！」孫悟空叫道。菩提祖師說：「天下無難事，只怕有心人。」接著他靠近孫悟空，悄悄地告訴他「筋斗雲」的咒語。不久，孫悟空就學會了。

Although Subodhi was pleased with Sun Wukong, he often saw flashes of cockiness. Subodhi warned him: "Never show off your powers, or they will get you in trouble." Sun Wukong promised he would not. But one day, while playing about with some students, Sun Wukong transformed himself into a pine tree, flaunting his powers. The ruckus brought Subodhi running from his cave. One look at the pine tree and he realized what had happened. "You broke your promise," Subodhi cried angrily. "Leave my cave!"

雖然菩提祖師對孫悟空很滿意，他也發現孫悟空經常得意忘形。他警告道：「千萬不要炫耀你的本領，那會替你帶來麻煩。」悟空答應祖師絕不炫耀。可是有一天，悟空和同學在玩耍時，為了要表現自己武功高強，他變成一棵松樹。同學的吵鬧聲驚動了菩提祖師，他從洞室跑出來，一看到松樹，就明白發生了什麼事。「你不遵守諾言，」祖師生氣地說：「離開這裡！」

Sun Wukong pleaded for another chance, but Subodhi would not be persuaded. "When you show off, people will ask you for the secret. Bad people will use it to harm others. And if you refuse to share your secrets, you could be harmed yourself. You have been here twenty years, and that is enough. Go back to your kingdom and use your powers to do good deeds."

悟空好後悔！他向老師求情：「請再給我一次機會！」祖師不答應，他說：「當你炫耀本領時，人家會求你教他。壞人學會了將去傷害別人。如果你不教他，他可能會想辦法傷害你。你在這裡已二十年，夠久了。回花果山吧！用你的本領去做好事。」

Although sad, Sun Wukong thanked his master for everything, recited the cloud-soaring spell, and flew off. In a twinkling, he was back at his beloved Flower Fruit Mountain. How strange that no one was there to greet him. He went to Water Curtain Cave and found everything lying in a broken heap. In a corner lay an old monkey who sobbed, "While you were away, Demon of Chaos came and took everyone away. I was so sick, they left me behind." Monkey King was furious, and he flew off to the Demon's cave.

孫悟空傷心地向老師道謝及告別。他唸起筋斗雲密語，一下子就飛得好遠。一眨眼功夫，他已回到心愛的花果山。奇怪！怎麼沒有朋友來迎接他呢？在水濂洞，他發現所有的東西都破成一堆堆的碎片，角落裡躺著一隻老猴子，一看到他就向他訴苦：「大王啊！當您不在時，混世魔王把大家都捉走了，我因為病重才留著。」美猴王氣壞了，他立刻飛去找魔王算賬。

"Come on out, Demon of Chaos!" Monkey King shouted. Hearing the challenge, the Demon quickly charged out of his cave, but seeing only a small monkey in front of him, he burst out laughing. How could one monkey fight a fearsome demon and his villainous crew? But in less than a blink of an eye, Monkey King flashed through the air, landing a stinging punch on the Demon's nose!

「滾出來！混世魔王！」美猴王大喊。魔王聽到外面的叫喊聲，立刻跑出來看，結果只看到一隻小猴子，他不禁大笑，一隻小猴子怎麼能和人見人怕的魔王和他兇勇的手下作戰？哇！魔王還沒笑完，孫悟空從空中一閃而過，狠狠地在魔王鼻子上揍了一拳！

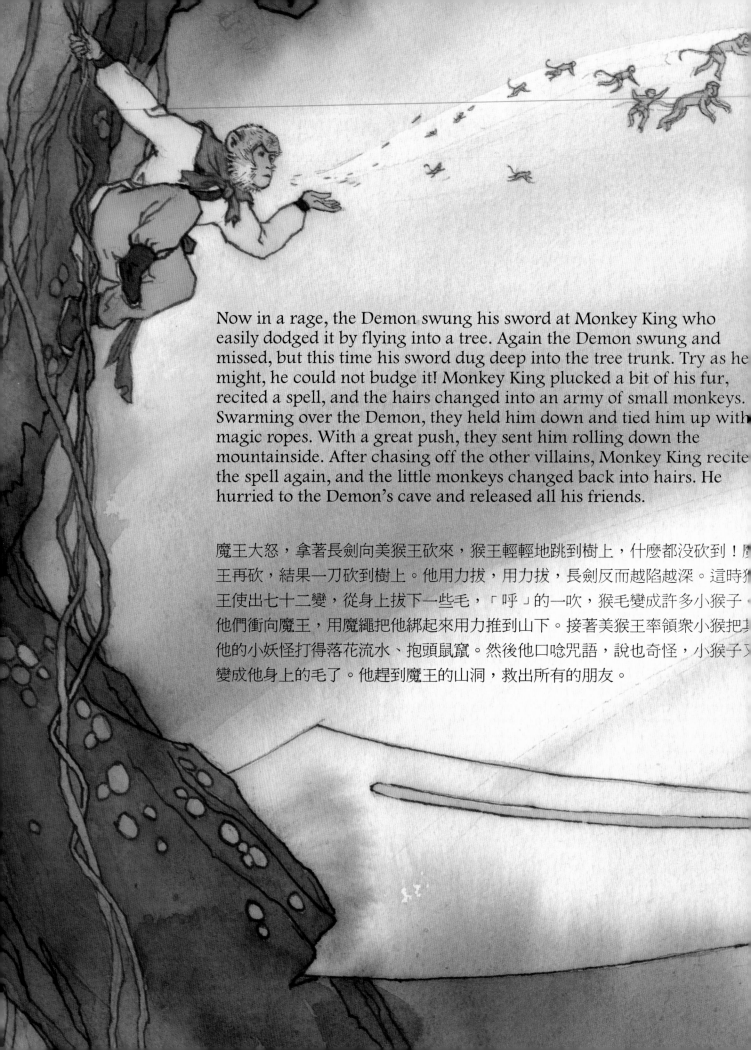

Now in a rage, the Demon swung his sword at Monkey King who easily dodged it by flying into a tree. Again the Demon swung and missed, but this time his sword dug deep into the tree trunk. Try as he might, he could not budge it! Monkey King plucked a bit of his fur, recited a spell, and the hairs changed into an army of small monkeys. Swarming over the Demon, they held him down and tied him up with magic ropes. With a great push, they sent him rolling down the mountainside. After chasing off the other villains, Monkey King recite the spell again, and the little monkeys changed back into hairs. He hurried to the Demon's cave and released all his friends.

魔王大怒，拿著長劍向美猴王砍來，猴王輕輕地跳到樹上，什麼都沒砍到！魔王再砍，結果一刀砍到樹上。他用力拔，用力拔，長劍反而越陷越深。這時猴王使出七十二變，從身上拔下一些毛，「呼」的一吹，猴毛變成許多小猴子。他們衝向魔王，用魔繩把他綁起來用力推到山下。接著美猴王率領眾小猴把其他的小妖怪打得落花流水、抱頭鼠竄。然後他口唸咒語，說也奇怪，小猴子又變成他身上的毛了。他趕到魔王的山洞，救出所有的朋友。

"Hurrah to our amazing Monkey King!" they cheered. Monkey King summoned the clouds, and carried his friends back to Water Curtain Cave. They celebrated their freedom and the return of their king with feasting and dancing for three days and three nights.

「美猴王萬歲！」他們高聲歡呼。美猴王召來一朵雲，大家一躍而上，駕雲飄回花果山水濂洞了。三天三夜，他們大吃大喝、唱歌跳舞，來慶祝重獲自由和大王遠遊歸來。

It was a glorious return for the Monkey King! But this, dear friends, is really just the beginning of many more adventures…

美猴王榮歸故里！但是親愛的小朋友們，真正精彩的故事還在後頭呢！

The Monkey King

In the seventh century, during the Tang dynasty, a Chinese Buddhist priest named Xuan Zang (c. 596-664) embarked on a dangerous pilgrimage to India to bring Buddhist scriptures back to China. The entire journey lasted twenty years. The priest returned to China in 645 bearing some six hundred texts and devoted the rest of his life to translating these into Chinese. In addition, he dictated a travelogue to a disciple and called it *The Tang Record of the Western Territories*. In it, he recounted details from his journey, the people he had met, and the harsh geography he survived (he scaled three of Asia's highest mountain ranges and nearly died of thirst on the desert plains).

Xuan Zang became a favorite of the Tang Emperor and a famous religious folk hero. For the next one thousand years the story of his pilgrimage inspired the literary imagination of storytellers and writers who embellished the journey with unbelievable episodes and fantastic characters drawn from popular folklore. In the thirteenth century, a supernatural monkey and pig became the priest's travel companions. Some scholars believe that the monkey may have been derived from Hanumat, the Monkey King from the Hindu tale, *Ramayana*. In the fourteenth century, a stage play in twenty-four scenes was composed. This drama is important because it contains all the main themes that would later appear in the sixteenth century Ming dynasty epic narrative *Journey to the West*.

Although written anonymously, there is much evidence showing that *Journey to the West* was most likely written around 1575 by a court official, poet and humor writer named Wu Cheng'en (c. 1500-82). The work is a massive, hundred-chapter masterpiece, and is more elaborate than any of the journey tales that came before it. It is not a novel in the conventional sense, but rather a complex narrative of episodic stories held together by the journey, its unifying motif. Wu Cheng'en did not merely weave the myriad tales together, he created a sophisticated allegory rich with humor, action, philosophy and satire. The mythical Monkey King who wreaks havoc in heaven, hell and everything in between, occupies the entire first part of Wu's epic. These first seven chapters are devoted to the beginnings of the Monkey King before his journey west: his birth and rise to kingship, his acquisition of magic under Master Subodhi, his gaining of immortality and disturbance of Heaven, and finally, his imprisonment under a mountain—the punishment set by the Buddha for his insolence. Throughout the remainder of the legend he consistently upstages the priest with his robust character and colorful antics.